Lizzie McGuire MYSTERIES

Case at CAMP GET-ME-OUTiE

By Lisa Banim

Based on the series

created by Terri Minsky

Watch it on

Disney CHANNEL

abc Kids

Disney PRESS

VOLO

New York

Printed in the United States of America

First Edition
1 3 5 7 9 10 8 6 4 2

Library of Congress Catalog Card Number: 2003112344

ISBN 0-7868-4621-6
For more Disney Press fun, visit www.disneybooks.com
Visit DisneyChannel.com

"So what'll it be?" Lizzie McGuire asked her best friend Miranda. "Strawberry wheatgrass kiwi or . . . strawberry wheatgrass kiwi?"

Miranda Sanchez wrinkled her nose as Lizzie poured the smoothie mixture out of the blender and into two tall glasses. "That looks totally gross," she said when Lizzie placed one of the glasses in front of her.

Lizzie sighed. "The color *is* a little weird," she admitted, examining her own glass.

"Lizzie, it looks like sludge," Miranda said.

"Must be the wheatgrass," replied Lizzie.

Mrs. McGuire came into the kitchen, balancing several bags of groceries. "Do my ears deceive me?" she said. "Are you kids actually having a snack that's *good* for you?"

Behind the counter, Lizzie's little brother held up his hands. "No way," said Matt. "I'm not ingesting *anything* involving Dr. Bubble Brain's experiments with food."

Lizzie glared at her brother. "Who asked you, pest?"

"You know, maybe it shouldn't even be ingested," said Matt. "Why don't you slap it on as a mask? Covering up *your* face seems like a beauty treatment to me."

"Be a good rodent and exterminate yourself," Lizzie told him. "There's nothing wrong with my face—or my smoothie recipe."

Miranda peered at her glass. "I don't know, Lizzie, those little kiwi seeds look like ants. No, wait a minute. They're moving! Maybe they *are* ants."

"Hey, wait a sec. That's actually sorta cool," Matt said. "Lemme see."

Lizzie shuddered, grabbed Miranda's glass, and quickly poured both smoothies down the drain.

Mrs. McGuire set down the groceries. "So," she said, "only sixty-four more days till school starts again. What are you kids planning to do this summer vacation?"

"Don't worry, Mom," Lizzie said. "Miranda and I have it all planned out."

Hanging out at the mall. Meeting cute guys at the pool. Catching a few rays. Now, *that's* a vacation!

"Yeah, we thought maybe we'd get some cool part-time jobs," Miranda said. "You know—low stress, high pay."

Mrs. McGuire raised one eyebrow. "Oh, really? Well, good luck with that, girls."

Just then, David Gordon knocked at the sliding glass door off the back deck. Mrs. McGuire waved for him to come in.

"Hey," he called, joining them in the kitchen.

"Hey, Gordo," Lizzie and Miranda said together, greeting their best friend.

"We were just discussing summer plans," Mrs. McGuire said. "So what will *you* be doing, Gordo?"

"Funny you should ask, Mrs. M," Gordo said. He spun around on his sneakers and pulled a brochure from his jeans pocket with an exaggerated flourish. "Voilà! My ticket to a thrill-packed, fun-filled week of discovery and adventure."

"What are you talking about?" Lizzie demanded.

"You're still hanging out with me and Miranda all summer, aren't you?"

"Maybe he's talking about an adventure park," Miranda said.

"Nope, even better." Gordo grinned. "I'm going to camp."

"What?" Lizzie said. "But, Gordo, you hate camping. Remember when we went on that overnight field trip for school?"

"Oh, but that was lots of fun, honey," Mrs. McGuire put in brightly. "Right?"

"Um, sure, Mom," Lizzie said exchanging glances with Miranda.

That trip would be forever burned in Lizzie's memory. Mrs. McGuire had volunteered to be the girls' chaperone—which had been majorly awkward. The boys had drenched all the girls with Super Soakers—which had been seriously immature. Their teacher had forced them to dig worms for the class worm farm—which had been totally gross. Then Lizzie's mom had led a toilet paper raid on the boys' tent—which had been totally embarrassing. "Fun" wasn't exactly the word Lizzie would have used to describe the experience.

"Well, this isn't just any camp," Gordo said. He held up the brochure. "It's Camp Bunsen Burner. Larry Tudgeman went last summer. He's been talking about it all year."

"Bunsen Burner?" Lizzie wrinkled her nose. "You mean, as in that, like, little silver thingy with the gas flame that we use to heat stuff up in science class?"

Matt grabbed the brochure from Gordo. "Whoa, science camp!" he said. "Cool! What do you get to blow up?"

"The experiments are all carefully controlled," Gordo said. Matt's face fell.

Mrs. McGuire peered over Matt's shoulder. "Well *I* think a fun, educational week at science camp is a great idea," she said. "And look, it says here that you can earn extra credit for school next fall."

No! No way! Don't even think about it! You'll never send me aliiiiiive. . . .

"Gee, that sounds great," Lizzie said, thinking fast. "*Except* that, you know, Miranda and I are going to be so busy with our . . . *volunteer* jobs—"

"Uh, right! At, um . . . at the library," said Miranda. She nodded. "Very educational."

"Mmmm," Mrs. McGuire said. She was still reading the brochure. "And they have a program for younger kids, too," she said. "Wonderful."

"Awesome!" Matt said. "I'll go find my sleeping bag." He bounded out of the kitchen.

This is *so* not happening, Lizzie thought, squeezing her eyes tightly. I refuse to spend an entire week of my summer vacation at Camp Geek.

"Hey, you guys should come, too," Gordo said to Lizzie and Miranda. "I bet you'd have a great time. Tudgeman says the place is totally cool."

"Right," Lizzie said, glaring at Gordo. "I'm sure."

Okay, Gordo, since when is Larry Tudgeman the official Grand Emperor of Cool? Did I miss something? Like a bunch of pigs flying?

"Back up," said Gordo. "You're totally focusing on the wrong guy here. *I'm* the one who thinks it's cool."

"You know, I just remembered something I have to do at home," Miranda said, hopping off her stool. "And it's really, really important. See ya."

"Bye," Lizzie said. But Gordo and her mom didn't even notice when Miranda left. They were too busy talking about what a great experience Lizzie would have at Camp Bunsen Burner.

Thanks a lot, Gordo, thought Lizzie.

Hello? Do I want to spend even one nanosecond of my summer vacation with flammable elements? Uh, *negative*!

One week later, Miranda and Lizzie found themselves in the parking lot of Hillridge Junior High, waiting to board the bus to science camp.

"I cannot believe we *both* have to go," complained Miranda. She kicked her large duffel bag with the toe of her black sneaker.

"I am so sorry, Miranda," said Lizzie. "If my mom hadn't called yours, you wouldn't be here waiting for the Geekland Express with me."

"It's *Gordo* who owes us big-time for this one," said Miranda.

"I know," said Lizzie. "But we can't be too hard on him. He really thinks we're all going to have a blast."

Miranda sighed. "I can't believe he played the parent card."

"It's like a conspiracy," Lizzie agreed. "There's no stopping the Mom Squad once they're on board."

"At least we'll have each other," said Miranda. "Besides, they can't turn us into science geeks in just one week." She suddenly went pale. "Can they?"

"Hope not," Lizzie said.

Mr. and Mrs. McGuire had dropped Lizzie and her spiky-haired excuse for a brother off bright and early. The Poster Child for Ugly was now hanging out with his equally annoying buddy Malina over by the buses.

Lizzie pulled her lime green sunglasses from the pocket of her yellow-plaid Capri pants. She shoved them on and looked around the sunny parking lot. There were parents and kids and counselors everywhere wearing totally bogus "Camp Bunsen Burner Ignites Summer Fun" T-shirts.

"Do you know any of these kids?" she asked Miranda.

"Nope," Miranda said. "Guess they're from other schools. . . ." She frowned at a boy walking past them with an armload of science textbooks and a butterfly net. "And possibly other planets."

"Hey, campers!" Gordo said, walking up to Lizzie and Miranda. He was lugging his sleeping bag, a duffel, his laptop computer and—strangely enough—a thick black leather briefcase with a black strap.

"Ready to hit the trail?" he asked.

Lizzie was about to tell Gordo that she was ready to hit *him*, when Miranda grabbed her arm.

"What?" Lizzie asked.

Miranda's mouth kept opening and closing, but no words were coming out.

"O-over th-there," she managed finally. "Major hottie sighting. *Really* major."

Lizzie followed Miranda's gaze. The term "hottie" was putting it mildly. The tall, buff, tanned sandy-haired guy with the clipboard was to die for—even if he was wearing a dorky Camp Bunsen Burner T-shirt. Not to mention, khaki shorts and a whistle.

Hmmm. A week in the woods at Camp-What's-its-Name is suddenly looking a whole lot better. Now, what's *his* name?

"He's seriously off the scale," Lizzie said dreamily.

Gordo threw up his hands. "He's a *counselor*. Completely off-limits."

"That's right, McGuire," snapped a girl's voice. "He's mine."

Lizzie whirled around. Kate Sanders, the Queen of Mean, was standing right behind her, looking perfect as usual in her white polo shirt, pressed khaki skirt, and diamond earrings. With her was Kate's best friend, Claire—royal runner-up to the Mean Queen. Her outfit was exactly the same as Kate's, except her polo shirt was pink.

Way back in grade school, Lizzie and Kate had actually been friends. That was hard for Lizzie to believe these days. Very hard.

"What are you guys doing here?" Miranda demanded. "Don't you have some cauldron full of frogs and eyeballs that needs stirring?"

Kate flipped her long blond hair over the shoulders of her white polo shirt. "As if," she said, "it's any of your business. But I need to pull up my science grade."

"Plus, there's a sports camp full of cute boys across the lake," Claire added. "That's reason enough for me."

Near the bus, an older man with wild white

hair and a white lab coat began waving his arms. "Let's go, science fans!" he called. "All aboard for Camp Bunsen Burner!"

"Remember, McGuire," Kate whispered nastily to Lizzie as she pushed past with her tennis racket, personal DVD player, and set of designer luggage. "The hottie counselor? Don't even think about it."

"All righty, then," Lizzie said with a sigh as she and Miranda followed Gordo and the others toward the buses to Camp Geek. "This is shaping up to be one unforgettably *miserable* week."

Lizzie and Miranda tried to get seats on the bus as far away as possible from Kate and Claire. The cheer-queen she-beasts were already enthroned in the last row.

"Lizzie, Lizzie, Lizzie," a familiar voice said as she sat down.

"Ethan?" Lizzie said in surprise. Ethan Craft had been her crush-boy since practically forever.

"I didn't know *you* were interested in . . . uh, science."

Ethan was definitely the cutest guy at Hillridge Junior High, no contest. He was also really cool. Just not always really bright.

"Me, neither," said Ethan, shrugging. He gave Lizzie and Miranda a sheepish grin. "I flunked science last term. It was this or summer school."

Excellent, Lizzie thought. Now there'll be *two* hotties at Camp Bunsen Burner. She smiled as the gorgeous counselor came down the aisle toward them.

Under her breath, Miranda began muttering, "Please sit near us, please sit near us."

But Mr. Hottie took a seat a few rows away, next to a pretty girl counselor. She had waist-length blond braids and wore a long, flowing skirt and a tie-dyed blouse. "Hi, I'm Sunny," Lizzie heard her say to a bunch of kids nearby. "I'm a Cancer. How about you guys? No, wait. Lemme guess."

"Spare us," Miranda whispered to Lizzie, rolling her eyes. "An astrology freak."

"Well, she looks nice, at least," Lizzie said as the bus pulled away from the school and turned onto the busy main road. "That guy in the lab coat up front seems kind of . . . odd."

Odd? Puh-leez.
He looks like a cross between an insane Albert Einstein and that weirdo professor guy from *Back to the Future!*

Suddenly, there was a shriek from the back of the bus. "Help!" someone screamed. "Get it away from me!"

Lizzie whipped around, along with everyone else on the bus.

Kate Sanders was plastered against the back windows. A chimp dressed in a Camp Bunsen Burner T-shirt had scampered up to her and was trying to offer her a banana.

"Stay back, you little hairy freak!" shrieked Kate.

The white-haired man in the lab coat hurried down the aisle of the moving bus. "Alonzo, get back here!" he cried. "Right now! Bad chimp!"

"Hey," Lizzie heard Matt say to Malina. The

two of them were sitting in front of her and Miranda. "He looks a lot like my chimp buddy, Fredo. Do you think maybe they're brothers?"

"Hmm," Malina said, tapping her chin thoughtfully. "Definitely a possibility." But Lizzie knew Malina wasn't thinking about the chimps being related. The sweet-looking blond with the budding criminal mind was always on the lookout for new ways to get Matt McGuire into trouble.

The man in the lab coat dragged Alonzo away from Kate. The chimp threw her a big smile over his shoulder as he was led back up the aisle.

"Sorry, everybody," the man said. "My little friend here doesn't always mind his manners. He's a primate in progress."

Dr. Weird chuckled at his own joke. So did a lot of the geeks.

A girl from another school with thick glasses and short, curly brown hair poked Lizzie's shoulder from behind and said, "You know, primate in progress. Like, evolution. Get it?"

Lizzie smiled weakly. "Um, right. Thanks."

Larry Tudgeman leaned across the aisle. "That's Professor Calvin," he told Miranda and Lizzie. "He's in charge of Camp Bunsen Burner. He's a brilliant animal behaviorist. He's trying to teach Alonzo to talk."

"Fascinating," Miranda said. She rolled her eyes at Lizzie.

The Tudge was sitting alone. Sort of. On the seat beside him was a huge, lumpy canvas duffel.

"What's in the bag, Larry?" Lizzie asked.

Tudgeman suddenly looked very nervous. He put both hands over the bag. "N-nothing," he said quickly. "It's none of your business."

Hey, like i actually *care!*

"That's your project for the science fair, isn't it?" said Gordo. He was sitting behind Lizzie and

20

Miranda, next to the girl with the thick glasses and short, curly hair.

Until Kate freaked, he'd had his nose in a book from the moment they'd sat down on the bus—*Chemistry for Life*. Lizzie shuddered.

"So what if it is my project?" Tudgeman shot back at Gordo. "I started it a little early to get a jump on the competition. It's top secret."

Miranda's eyes narrowed. "Whoa, wait a minute. Gordo, did you say 'science fair'?"

Gordo nodded. "Sure. The Camp Bunsen Burner Science Expo is the highlight of the week. They have one every summer. Camper participation is required."

"WHAT?!" Lizzie and Miranda both said in horror.

"I was runner-up last year," Tudgeman bragged. "My name was in *Future Scientists of America* magazine."

"Big whoop," Gordo said. But Lizzie could tell he was ferociously jealous.

"This is so unfair," Miranda protested. "No one said anything about having to do any projects. That's like . . . *school* or something."

"No," Lizzie said. "It's much, much worse."

On the other hand, spending all those long, endless hours by the light of a flickering Bunsen burner might be fun. With lots of extra help from a certain hottie science counselor, of course. . . .

Matt leaned over the back of his seat and told Lizzie, "Guess you didn't read the fine print, sister dearest."

His grubby little hand shoved the Camp Bunsen Burner brochure under Lizzie's nose. "Check it out," he said. "There's a major cash prize—*and* a profile of the winner in *Future*

Scientists of America magazine. Malina and I are entering for sure."

"Whatever," Lizzie said.

Gordo and Tudgeman were starting to bicker now. "Fine," Gordo said. "If you're not revealing your project, then I'm not, either."

Tudgeman frowned. "You started one already, too?"

"Did I start my project?" Gordo said loudly. He stood up for dramatic effect. "Ha! I have discovered a chemical formula that will change the future of mankind!"

Everyone on the bus turned to stare at Gordo. He smiled nervously and lifted up the thick black leather briefcase he'd brought along. "And it's right in *here*."

Just then, the hottie counselor headed down the aisle. "Hey, buddy," he said to Gordo in a deep, friendly voice. "You've got to sit down while the bus is moving, okay? We don't want anyone getting hurt."

Lizzie stared up at Mr. Hottie. It was so nice of him to be concerned about Gordo's safety. So responsible, so *mature*. Mr. Hottie here would never Super Soak a bunch of girls—like that hoodlum pack of junior high infants.

"McGuire," Lizzie heard Kate threaten from the back of the bus. Queen Mean obviously meant business about staking out Mr. Hottie for herself.

Then the hippie counselor with the braids came to join Mr. Hottie. "Hi, there," she said. "I haven't met you guys yet. I'm Sunny Novak, the girls' head counselor. I thought it would be really neat to introduce ourselves by our astrological signs." She looked straight at Gordo. "I bet I can guess yours."

Gordo quickly sat down. "I don't believe in that stuff," he said. "I'm a scientist."

"Oh, me too," Sunny said, smiling. "And you know what? I have this month's star charts for every sign in the zodiac right here in this bag. If you want I can—"

Suddenly, Lizzie smelled something foul. She quickly covered her nose. The bus was filling up with bright pink smoke!

"Stop the bus!" Professor Calvin shouted to the driver. "We're going to evacuate! Everybody close your eyes and hold on to the person in front of you as you exit the bus."

The bus lurched to a halt. All the kids began coughing and sputtering as they hurried quickly toward the emergency doors.

"Do not panic!" Professor Calvin called. "There is no need to be alarmed. It is a perfectly inert and nontoxic gas. I repeat, do not panic!"

Lizzie grabbed Miranda's hand and followed the other campers off the bus. The smoke smelled like some kind of . . . stink bomb.

Welcome to my summer vacation, thought Lizzie in disgust.

Now, will somebody please get me *outie* here?!

"Aaaaaagh!" Lizzie gulped for air as she and the rest of the Camp Bunsen Burner inmates escaped the stinky smoke that had filled up the bus.

"That was *so* gross!" she cried.

"Tell me about it," Miranda said, coughing.

Lizzie looked around to make sure Matt was okay. Her brother seemed just fine. He was standing outside, under one of the bus windows, gazing up in awe. The vile pink smoke was still pouring out.

"Amazing," Matt said to Malina. "I have to find out how to make this stuff. It'll be great for the school cafeteria."

Professor Calvin and a bunch of counselors were bustling around the groups of kids, checking to make sure they were all okay.

"No cause for alarm, boys and girls," Professor Calvin told them. "The gas is just a basic mixture of two quite harmless elements." He chuckled. "Looks like someone's wasting no time with the science pranks."

"Prank?" Kate said indignantly. "This is *sooo* not funny. My hair is going to smell like rotten eggs."

For once I have to agree with Kate. We're not even to camp yet and it already stinks!

"Who would do such a stupid thing?" Miranda said to Lizzie.

"I don't know," Lizzie answered. "But Professor Calvin sure seems calm about it. He even seems sort of . . . amused."

"He probably did it himself," Miranda said. "You know, to show us all how totally fun science can be."

Just then, the hottie counselor stepped off the bus. "All clear!" he announced.

"Excellent," Professor Calvin said. "We'll wait a minute or two to make sure all the smoke is gone. In the meantime, boys and girls, let me take this unexpected opportunity to introduce your Camp Bunsen Burner staff."

He waved toward Counselor Hottie. "This is Devon Adams, the head boys' counselor."

Devon smiled and waved. All the girls, especially Lizzie, swooned. Even the she-geeks looked interested.

"Devon just published a paper in *American*

Scientific Journal as a freshman at Valley Tech," Professor Calvin added.

There were gasps of admiration from the she-geek section.

Wow. So, Devon is gorgeous *and* brilliant. Sorry, Ethan—I may just have a new crush-boy for this trip!

"Pretty impressive, *American Scientific Journal*," Gordo said as he walked up to Lizzie and Miranda. He had finally found them in the crowd.

Tudgeman was right on Gordo's heels. "I have my own subscription," he bragged.

Lizzie noticed that Gordo was still carrying his precious black leather briefcase. And Tudgeman was lugging his mysterious duffel.

Professor Calvin nodded to Sunny Novak. "Most of you have already met Sunny, our girls' head counselor," he said. "Sunny has fashioned a rather unique major for herself at Silver Beach College."

"I'm a galactic studies specialist," Sunny said.

"Huh?" Gordo said in a low voice. "How can you *specialize* in the *galaxy?*"

"Shh," Miranda told him.

Professor Calvin introduced more counselors. But Lizzie wasn't paying attention. She was too busy watching Devon. He was chatting with some of the younger campers.

When Lizzie finally emerged from her bliss fog, she noticed Sunny talking to Gordo. The counselor seemed to be asking him a bunch of questions. Then she searched through a stack of cards in her bag.

"What's she up to?" Lizzie asked Miranda.

Miranda shrugged. "I guess she's showing kids their star charts."

"Oh," Lizzie said. Gazing at star charts was far less interesting to her than gazing at Devon.

She jumped when Professor Calvin clapped his hands. "Okay, science fans," he said. "Back on the bus!"

"Do we have to?" Miranda complained.

"Miranda," said Lizzie, pulling her friend aside, "I think we need to stay focused on the *positive* aspects of this experiment."

Miranda followed Lizzie's gaze to Devon. "Gotcha," she agreed. "Let's go."

Everyone piled onto the bus again. Gordo and Tudgeman seemed unfazed by the lingering smell.

"Stink bomb," Gordo said, shrugging.

"Amateurs," Tudgeman said.

Lizzie and Gordo sat together this time. But Gordo and Tudgeman never took their eyes off each other across the aisle.

Then Gordo turned to Lizzie. In a low voice, he said, "You know, I could have sworn I felt someone trying to grab my briefcase as we were evacuating the bus." He tapped the black briefcase on his lap. "It's a very good thing I was holding tight to this baby."

Lizzie shook her head. "Gordo, do you really think someone would *want* it?" She frowned. "When did you start carrying that thing, anyway?"

"Shh!" Gordo said. He glanced around them. "What I told everyone before the smoke bomb went off was the truth. This briefcase contains notes for my secret formula."

Maybe Gordo was just being paranoid. But she had to admit, the timing of the stink bomb was a teeny bit suspicious. Had someone set it off as a *prank*—or as a *distraction*?

The Camp Bunsen Burner Science Expo was coming up in a week. And Gordo had announced to the whole bus that he had some majorly important scientific discovery inside that briefcase.

Hmmm . . . Lizzie decided to keep her eyes open, just in case. After all, this science-fair thing was really important to Gordo.

Guard someone with an important black briefcase? Hey, i wonder if i'll have a future in the Secret Service.

CHAPTER

5

Half an hour later, the bus turned off the high-way onto a long dirt road. It bumped along and finally stopped beside a broken wooden sign. The only thing visible, besides the sign, was a thick tangle of trees, bushes, and overgrown weeds.

"I'd turn back if I were you," Miranda cackled in a Wicked Witch of the West voice.

"What kind of camp is this?" Lizzie asked, peering out the bus window. "There's nothing here."

"Everyone off the bus!" Professor Calvin said cheerfully. "We're going to hike down to the cabin area."

"Can we see the lab first?" one of the kids asked. A glare from Kate quickly shut the poor geek up.

"Where's the lake?" Claire asked. "And how far across is that boys' sports camp?"

"Well, now," Professor Calvin said. "The lab is over there through the woods a ways. And as for your question, young lady, the distance can be calculated by several different ways of measurement. Using the metric system, for example—"

"Never mind, thanks," Claire snapped.

As the kids got off the bus, Devon, Sunny, and a red-haired counselor with a smiley-face name tag that said MARSHA handed out Camp Bunsen Burner caps. Then they all began hiking down the hill. Alonzo the chimp scampered beside Professor Calvin, who told them the camp rules along the way.

"Lights out at nine?" Miranda complained to Lizzie. "And breakfast at seven? But this is our vacation! He's kidding, right?"

"I don't think so." Lizzie sighed.

"And now for your cabin assignments," Professor Calvin announced when they reached the bottom of the hill. A long row of tiny log cabins stretched all the way to the muddy-looking lake.

"Hey!" Miranda said, frowning. "That sign says, 'No Swimming.'"

"Correct. We've been conducting a very interesting algae study," Professor Calvin informed her.

Miranda shook her head in disgust.

Then the professor began reading kids' names off his clipboard. All of the cabins were identified by chemical compounds. Gordo and Tudgeman were in Devon's cabin: Potassium Chloride.

Lizzie and Miranda were assigned to Silver Nitrate, Sunny's cabin. Also in Lizzie's cabin were

Judy, the girl from the bus with the thick glasses and curly hair; and Trudy, a shy she-geek friend of Judy's.

And, of course, Kate and Claire.

> The scientific probability of my being stuck in a cabin with those two highly predictable elements? Easy. One hundred percent.

Lizzie and Miranda followed Sunny and the she-geeks to their cabin. Silver Nitrate was totally falling apart. The window screens had gigantic holes in them.

"It's dark in here," Miranda said. "Where's the light switch?"

"There isn't one," Sunny said cheerfully. "The cabins don't have electricity. Pretty cool, huh?"

Kate swept past Lizzie, Miranda, Judy, and

Trudy. "The bottom bunk over there is mine," she said. "It's the only one with a halfway decent-looking mattress."

She threw her designer luggage on the bed—and let out a bloodcurdling scream!

Lizzie ran across the cabin. "Kate, what's wrong?" she said.

Sunny was right behind her. "Yeah, are you okay?"

Kate was still screaming hysterically and pointing at the bed.

Lizzie looked over Kate's shoulder. Lying on the bed was a glass jar with something slimy-looking inside. "Gross," she said. She reached out and gingerly picked up the jar.

"Well, what is it?" Claire demanded, coming up.

Slowly, Lizzie turned the jar around. The hideous slimy thing revolved in the liquid inside the jar. "It's . . . some kind of pickled frog or something." She shuddered. "Ewww."

"Hmm," Sunny said. "That's a dissection specimen from the bio lab. It's preserved in formaldehyde. Wonder how that got in here."

Yeah, me too. But ten points for whoever sent Kate ballistic like that. Coolie!

Kate recovered herself quickly. "Well, someone get it *out* of here," she said, crossing her arms. "Like, right *now*."

One of their she-geek cabin mates—Judy—reached out eagerly. "I'll take it."

"Wait," Lizzie said. She looked at the gross jar more closely. The frog's eyes stared back at her. "There's another label pasted over the first one. It says—" She frowned. "Gordon, David."

Sunny put her hands to the sides of her forehead. "I'm getting a familiar aura here. Gordon . . . Gordon . . ."

Kate pointed at the jar. "Okay, McGuire," she said. "Enough for the Ms. Helpful Act. Your little friend Gor-dork put you up to this, didn't he?"

"Me?" Lizzie said. "Kate, I didn't leave this jar there. And neither did Gordo. He and Tudgeman went to check out the lab as soon as we got here. And besides, why would Gordo leave something like this with his name on it?"

"Let's just see if he did, shall we?" Kate said. She grabbed the jar from Lizzie and stomped out the door.

Lizzie and the others followed her. "Kate, think about it," she said. "How could anyone have known you'd pick that bunk?"

"Oh, puh-leez," Kate said in disgust. "Like there was any other choice."

Just then, Devon came up behind them. "Hey, what's going on?" he asked. "Is everything okay?"

"No, it's *not* okay!" Kate whirled around. But when she saw Devon, her angry frown disappeared.

She smiled sweetly. "I mean, sure, everything's fine. Now that *you're* here to help us."

Whoa. I'm surprised Kate didn't get whiplash from reversing herself so fast. That girl is phonier than the plants in my dentist's office!

Kate held out the frog jar. "I found this really scary thing in my bed," she said.

Devon chuckled. "Well, don't worry," he said. "That frog isn't going anywhere." He took the jar from Kate. "Except straight back to the lab where he belongs."

There was a sudden commotion from the cabin behind them—shouts and loud voices. It was from Potassium Chloride, Gordo's cabin.

Sunny held out her arms and closed her eyes. "I'm sensing a disturbance," she said.

Everyone rushed to Potassium Chloride. Sunny's not the only one getting a bad feeling, thought Lizzie as she walked toward the dark doorway. "Gordo?" she called into the cabin.

Her friend was standing beside his bunk, surrounded by a bunch of other guys. He was clutching his briefcase and a large piece of black cardboard.

Some of Gordo's cabin mates were laughing. But Gordo wasn't. Neither was Larry Tudgeman. He was standing by his bunk, guarding his mysterious duffel bag.

"Check this out," Gordo said to Lizzie. "I found it on top of my duffel bag when I got back from the lab."

Lizzie looked over his shoulder. The piece of cardboard looked like some kind of map. It was covered with little white dots and numbers. Someone had written *GORDON, DAVID* in big, red letters at the top of the card. A date was circled, and next to the date was a message in the same angry, red handwriting: YOUR STARS POINT TO DOOM.

Lizzie shuddered when she read the message.

"Where did you get that?" Sunny asked Gordo. She looked disturbed.

"Someone left it on top of my duffel bag," Gordo explained.

Sunny took the chart and studied it. "This is mine. I developed the whole system myself. Someone must have stolen this from my tote bag on the bus."

Gordo gulped. "What does it mean?" he asked Sunny.

But it was Lizzie who replied. "Gordo, you don't believe in any of that astrology stuff, anyway. Remember?"

Me, neither. Unless the stars say that a tall, handsome, brilliant counselor is about to fall in love with me.

"Um, right," Gordo said. "I'm a scientist."

"Well, the study of star patterns and their relation to all natural beings is a science, too," Sunny said. "In fact, my galactic studies major is a special application of astronomy and psychology."

"Fascinating," Lizzie heard Tudgeman say.

"And Gordo's *real* stars look fine," Sunny added. "Or, at least . . . they're not *that* bad."

"So why did someone circle that date and write that stuff about my stars pointing to doom?" asked Gordo.

This time, Devon spoke up. "This is obviously another prank," he said, putting a hand on Gordo's shoulder. "You know, like that smoke bomb on the bus."

"Sounds more like a warning," said Miranda.

"Yeah," said Tudgeman. "And note the date. It's Saturday—the day of the Science Expo."

"And what about *this*," Kate said. She pointed to the jar with the pickled frog. "Hello? This has your name on it, Gordon. *Literally.* You owe me an explanation. So start talking."

Just then, a loud, scratching sound filled the cabin. A tape-recorded bugle began to play.

"Hey, it's time for dinner," Devon said, moving toward the cabin door. "We'll all feel better if we have something to eat. Let's head up to the dining hall and talk about this stuff later."

Everyone followed Devon out the door—except Lizzie, Gordo, and Miranda.

"Don't worry, Gordo," Sunny said on her way out. She gave him a reassuring smile. "Your *real* stars are fine. That's the important thing. Miranda was right. It's just some kind of a warning."

"Gee, thanks, that makes me feel *so* much better," muttered Gordo.

"All I'm saying is, you can't hold it against the galaxy," said Sunny. "I certainly can't. *My* stars are pointing to an extreme power and energy field right now. Peace out!"

Someone has been doing a little too much yoga. Scientific fact: those wacky yoga positions also contort the brain.

"That is one strange babe," Miranda said, as Sunny disappeared in a flash of purple tie-dye.

"Mmmm," Lizzie said. Strange wasn't the word Lizzie had in mind. More like *suspicious.*

She couldn't wait to start a detective notebook on this case after dinner. She was now sure that someone was after Gordo.

And his formula.

Could Tudgeman have planted the smoke bomb and the frog and the star chart? He was determined to win the Camp Bunsen Burner Science Expo. And he'd been sticking to Gordo—and Gordo's briefcase—like glue. Was he trying to scare Gordo out of entering the competition? Or into leaving the camp entirely?

Then there was Sunny Novak. Lizzie had no idea what kind of motive the spacey girls' counselor would have to steal Gordo's formula. But Sunny always seemed to be popping up when anything weird happened. And the star chart had come from *her* bag.

But maybe that was a little too obvious, thought Lizzie. Like, maybe someone was trying to frame Sunny. On the other hand, Sunny could have set it all up to make it *look* like someone had stolen it from her bag—just so no one would suspect her. *Hmmmm . . .*

Note to self: look for a possible motive for Sunny. Detective forecast: she may not be so . . . Sunny.

Miranda sighed. "We might as well get dinner," she said. "I'm starving."

"Let's boogie," Gordo said. He picked up his briefcase from the bunk.

"Are you really going to take your briefcase to the dining hall?" Lizzie asked.

"I'm going to have this thing with me twenty-four/seven," Gordo declared as the three of them left Potassium Chloride. "Even if I have to sleep with it."

"Well, no worries," Lizzie told him. "I promise you, Gordo, your formula for the Science Expo is safe now that I'm on the case."

Um . . . at least i hope so.

CHAPTER

6

"**T**his place is so weird," Lizzie said as she and her friends walked into the Camp Bunsen Burner dining hall. She tried to ignore the stuffed woodland creatures on the ledge over the door.

"I can't believe they actually serve food in here," Miranda said. "It smells like something's rotting."

"Hey, I think it's pretty cool," Gordo said. "Check out that old science equipment in the case over there. I bet that microscope belonged to Louis Pasteur. You know, the guy who brought us pasteurized milk."

"Spare us, Gordo," Lizzie told him. "We've had enough science today."

She plastered herself against the wall as Professor Calvin zoomed past with Alonzo. The chimp was carrying a plate of bananas.

"Having fun, campers?" Professor Calvin asked.

"Oh, tons," Lizzie said, smiling. Miranda winced and nodded.

"You have to admit," Gordo said when the professor and his chimp were gone. "That garden we saw outside had some awesome-looking veggies. Someone must be studying genetics."

Miranda's mouth dropped open. "They're serving us *experimental* food?" she cried.

And i thought school cafeteria meals were bad. At least phony cafeteria cheese doesn't mess with your DNA!

Lizzie looked around the large dining hall. Campers were sitting at long tables, telling science jokes and exchanging trivia. Matt was the center of attention at one table. He was pulling a strand of spaghetti out of his nose.

You owe me *so* big-time, Mom, Lizzie thought. This is a whole week of my life I'll never get back.

She picked up a tray and followed Miranda and Gordo through the food line.

"Hi, there," a deep, friendly voice said. "You're Lizzie, right?"

Lizzie almost dropped her tray. Devon was standing there in all his tanned, sandy-haired, athletic glory. He was smiling at her. And he actually knew her name!

"Sure," said Lizzie. "I think so. I mean, yes."

"Why don't you and your friends join us at our table?" he said. "We have room."

"Great," Lizzie said. She couldn't help feeling

a little smug as she walked past Kate with her tray. He likes me! she thought.

Here's my chance to show Devon my brilliant scientific mind. What was Gordo saying about that milk pasture guy?

When Lizzie, Gordo, and Miranda reached Devon's table, Ethan and Tudgeman were already there.

"Hey, guys, what's up?" said Ethan.

"Hi, Ethan," Lizzie said, sitting down with her tray. It was hard for her to believe, but Ethan didn't seem quite as amazing next to Devon.

Ethan turned back to Tudgeman. "So, like I was saying, dude, I need a serious favor. How about if I become, like, your assistant for the Science Expo?"

"No, thanks," Tudgeman said. He patted the

duffel sitting next to him. "I work alone."

Ethan dipped a french fry into some tartar sauce. "I really need a decent grade to pass science this year," he said. "And I don't have a project yet. I won't mess yours up or anything."

"Don't bet on it," Gordo muttered. Lizzie nudged him and frowned.

Ethan pushed his plate of french fries toward Tudgeman. "Like, please?"

Tudgeman picked up a fry. "Well . . ." he said slowly. "I *suppose* I could find a use for an assistant, IF you put in a good word for me with Kate. I'm far too busy for romantic entanglements right now. So please speak to her when we get back to school."

"Done and done, dude," said Ethan.

"So, what kind of project is the Tudge here working on?" Gordo asked Ethan casually.

"Yes, tell us about it," said Devon. "I'm always interested in hearing about camper projects, and I'm happy to help out if I can."

"Oh, I saw it in the bathroom," Ethan began. "It's this really cool—"

Tudgeman jumped up and threw out his hands like a policeman. "Ethan, stop right there!" he said. "Rule number one for being my assistant is keeping your lips zipped."

Larry made a dorky gesture of "zipping" closed his lips, then throwing away an imaginary key.

Why is Tudgeman such a . . . Tudgeman?

"No problemo, boss," Ethan said. He shrugged at Gordo and Devon. "Sorry, dudes."

The rest of dinner was a blur for Lizzie. She remembered Gordo holding his briefcase the whole time he was eating and yakking with Tudgeman about the experimental veggies. But mostly Lizzie remembered staring at Devon. He's so deelish, she told herself dreamily.

At least there's *something* worth sticking around this place for. Uh, besides protecting Gordo and his formula, of course!

* * *

That night, Lizzie lay awake in her bunk. She couldn't seem to get to sleep after a thrilling night around a campfire buzzing with mosquitoes. Not to mention a few science lectures and several rounds of the Camp Bunsen Burner song led by Sunny on folk guitar.

Lizzie took her flashlight and her detective notebook out from under her mattress. It was just a blank school notebook she'd brought along, but it would serve her purposes nicely. She needed to organize her thoughts about the case—and writing things down always helped.

But as she uncapped her purple pen, she heard a strange, whirring sound from the woods outside.

What is *that*? she wondered.

Lizzie shrugged and turned back to her notebook. Then she heard a scratching noise at the screen next to her bunk. *Yikes!* Lizzie thought. She poked Miranda's mattress above her. "Miranda?" she called.

Her best friend was snoring. Loudly. All the other girls in the cabin were sleeping, too. Kate was wearing a frilly satin eye mask.

The noise came again, louder this time. Lizzie gulped and looked through the screen. Someone—or something—was definitely out there.

Gathering her courage, Lizzie lit one of the cabin's rusty red lanterns and walked outside in her pajamas.

It was only Gordo!

Lizzie sagged against the side of the cabin in relief. "You scared me to death," she told him.

Gordo held out both arms. "Look!" he said. "One is normal, and the other is covered in bug bites."

"Great. Thanks for sharing," Lizzie said. "Good night, Gordo." She turned to go back inside.

"No, wait!" Gordo said. "I did a test run of my secret formula. It totally repels mosquitoes. And get this—I just figured out how to make it glow in the dark. You can even use it in a cabin with no electricity!"

"That's nice, Gordo," Lizzie said sleepily.

Suddenly, a tall dark shadow stepped out from behind a large rock—and walked toward Lizzie and Gordo!

S tay calm, Lizzie told herself as the dark figure drew closer to her and Gordo. Every camp horror movie she'd ever seen flashed through her mind.

"Who is it?" Gordo called into the woods. Then he turned to Lizzie and whispered, "Give me your lantern, quick."

Lizzie handed him the rusty red lantern, and Gordo began to walk toward the dark figure.

That's when the dark shape switched on a flashlight. "Okay, you two," a deep voice said. "Back in your cabins, on the double."

Devon? *Phew!* Not a psycho stalker. Then Lizzie came to her senses. *Devon!* She crossed her arms over her oversized flannel pajamas.

Darn, thought Lizzie. Why does Devon have to see me in these? They look like Gammy McGuire's rejects.

Lizzie had *wanted* to buy a pair of silk baby-doll pj's, but her Mom had nixed that idea. Thanks again, Mom, she thought.

"Oh, hi, Devon. What are you doing here?" Lizzie asked.

"I'm on night duty," Devon said. "I make sure everyone is safe and sound." He grinned. "Come on, Gordo, I'll take you back to the guys' side."

Gordo handed Lizzie back her lantern.

"You could have kept your flashlight on," Lizzie heard Gordo grumble to Devon as the counselor escorted him toward Cabin Potassium Chloride. "You kind of freaked us out sitting there in the dark like that."

"Well, I didn't want to keep anyone awake, leaving my light on," Devon said.

"Bye," Lizzie called into the darkness. Devon was so deelish, she thought. And nice, too. Maybe tomorrow she could tell him about her worries that someone was after Gordo's project.

Then again, he might just think she was being silly and totally overreacting. After all, from his point of view, this stuff probably did look like a bunch of harmless pranks.

Were they? she wondered.

As Lizzie turned to go into her cabin, a movement caught the corner of her eye. She gasped.

A ghostlike figure was moving along the dark path near the younger kids' cabins.

Lizzie raised her lantern higher, ready to scream for help. Then she narrowed her eyes.

The ghost was short and pale and spiky-headed. *Matt!*

Lizzie marched toward her brother. As she got closer, she saw that he was muttering to himself. Was he sleepwalking? she wondered

Worried, Lizzie ran and grabbed Matt's arm. But she'd read somewhere that you should never wake a sleepwalker. Too late.

"Hey, let go of me!" Matt said.

"What are you doing out here?" Lizzie demanded.

"I'm looking for the ghost of the creepy caretaker," Matt said. "This place is haunted. Remember the story that guy told us at the campfire?"

After dinner, the campers had assembled for a lecture on combustion. The result was a campfire. Then they got a lecture on flammable elements. The result was a bizarre display of flammable elements in action—which looked sort of like neon fireworks.

The story about the caretaker drowning in the lake and his ghost terrorizing campers was told to them after all the science lectures—just for "fun." Lizzie couldn't believe her brother believed it.

"Oh, puh-leez," Lizzie said. "You've seen too many horror movies with Dad."

"Matt McGuire!" a girl's shrill voice called. Lizzie and her brother both jumped. Matt's buddy Malina stepped out of the darkness.

"What's she doing here?" Lizzie asked.

"We were supposed to have a secret meeting in the woods," said Matt, "but I sorta got distracted with my ghost hunt."

"What do you think you're doing wandering around the woods like a pinhead?" Malina asked Matt, hands on her hips. "You're wasting precious time! Now, let's get to work."

Then Malina spun around and marched back into the shadows.

"Coming, my angel," Matt called. "Gotta go," he told Lizzie. "I can't keep my science partner waiting. We're going to win that grand prize, and it's gonna be a rough road, lemme tell ya. I've got some whiz kid in my cabin—Jake Novak. His sister helped him start sketching his project out last

Labor Day weekend, so we have a lot of catching up to do."

"His sister?" said Lizzie.

"Yeah, Sunny Novak. Hello? Your counselor? Too bad *my* sister isn't a science brainiac—but I'll muddle through without your help *somehow*."

Sunny a brainiac? Lizzie squeezed her eyes tightly as Matt ran off.

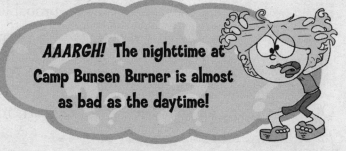

AAARGH! The nighttime at Camp Bunsen Burner is almost as bad as the daytime!

For a nanosecond, Lizzie worried that she and Miranda didn't have a project idea yet. Tomorrow would be their first day in the lab.

Oh, who cares? Lizzie told herself as she finally walked back into Cabin Silver Nitrate. My project is making sure Gordo's project stays safe. And right now I need some sleep.

But Lizzie tossed and turned, thinking about the case. She propped herself up on one elbow and looked over at Sunny's bunk.

Their counselor had meditated herself to sleep. She even kept a little battery-operated fountain on the floor next to her bed to help her "dreams remain serene," as she put it.

Could Sunny want Gordo's secret formula? Lizzie wondered. But why? Sunny probably didn't even know what it was, unless she'd been snooping through Gordo's notes.

And who else would know about star charts? Of course, someone may have used the charts to *frame* Sunny, too. *Hmmm . . .*

On the other hand, Sunny was always around whenever something went wrong. And waitie just a second! Matt had said she'd helped her little brother with his science fair project. Was she worried about Gordo stealing Jake's thunder? *Whoa.* That was definitely a motive.

Then again, what if Sunny was innocent?

Who else could be after Gordo's formula? What about Devon?

But why? He was so nice and incredibly gorgeous and helpful and brilliant. He had already been published in that big-time impressive scientific journal. Why in the world would he care about a junior-high kid's science project?

Lizzie sighed and rolled over. For some reason, Professor Calvin popped into her mind next. He'd acted a little strangely during the smoke incident on the bus. But he hadn't seemed to be around for the frog jar or the star chart threat. And he didn't have a motive, either. Why would he hurt the reputation of his own camp?

Unless . . . Lizzie sat up in bed. Maybe he wanted to kill the camp's reputation by making it look like there was doom and danger here. Maybe he wanted to make the camp owners sell the place to him! That was always a big Nancy Drew book motive. Maybe there was some long-forgotten treasure buried at Camp Bunsen Burner. Or oil underneath it.

Ha! Are you kidding? There's nothing valuable here. This place is a total dump!

And then there was Tudgeman . . . He *definitely* wanted to beat Gordo in the Science Expo. But he always seemed to have an alibi. He was never out of Gordo's sight—and vice versa.

Lizzie punched her pillow in frustration. Finally, she gave up and began to drift off to sleep. Until she heard that bizarre-o whirring noise outside again. Something was crashing around in the bushes!

Okay, that's it! Lizzie thought. She jumped up and ran to the door—just in time to see Larry Tudgeman fleeing through the trees.

"Aha!" Lizzie said out loud. "Bingo!"

She was almost through the door when she felt a hand on her shoulder.

"You can't go out there, Lizzie," Sunny said. Her blond hair glowed in the moonlight and her pupils were so dilated they made her eyes seem almost totally black. "There's a very disturbing presence."

"How come you're awake?" Lizzie asked with a shudder. The counselor had slept through everything else—or at least Lizzie had *thought* she'd been sleeping. Could Sunny have been *pretending* to sleep all along, but secretly listening to her and Gordo?

Sunny smiled. "Oh, that rainfall fountain next to my bed is great to fall asleep to," she explained. "But I wake up having to use the little girls' cabin a lot. Now, back to bed with you."

Lizzie sighed in frustration as she headed to her bunk. Tudgeman had gotten away.

The next morning at breakfast, Lizzie made sure she sat next to Tudgeman and his duffel bag.

"Oh, hi, Larry," she said. "Did you sleep okay?"

Tudgeman frowned at her. "Does it *look* like it?"

"Not really," Lizzie said. There were big, dark circles under his eyes. And he definitely sounded grumpy. She turned to Tudgeman's new assistant. "And how did *you* sleep, Ethan?" she asked.

"Like a rock," Ethan said.

"Hard to believe," Gordo said, opening a package of Frootie Crunch.

"So are you guys all ready to hit the lab today?" Lizzie asked brightly. "I bet you can't wait to work on those projects." She stared straight at Tudgeman. Did he know she'd seen him last night in the woods?

"Lizzie, did anyone ever tell you that you're way too perky in the morning?" Tudgeman asked.

Me? PERKY? i am *so* not the Katie Couric type! Who could ever get up at four every morning, anyway? Even with a bugle. Um, can i please have another shot of espresso? (Oh, yeah, i don't drink coffee. i was too tired to remember that.)

"Hey!" Gordo said. "What's your problem, Tudgeman?" He wiggled his eyebrows. "Pressure getting to you?"

"Whoa, guys," Devon broke in. "Take it easy, okay?"

What a cool guy Devon is, Lizzie thought. So diplomatic. But it was nice of Gordo to defend me. And Tudgeman is a nervous wreck. He's in my Number One Suspect slot for sure.

Just then, Professor Calvin stepped to the center of the room. He held up his hand for silence.

"Listen up, campers," he said. "I have an important announcement to make."

Miranda finally looked up from her grapefruit. "Camp Bunsen Burner is closing?" she muttered hopefully. "How about a snow day?"

"We have a very special all-camp activity planned this morning," the professor went on. "A one-hundred-percent-scientific scavenger hunt!"

A buzz began to rise through the dining hall.

Some of the kids did not sound happy.

"This means, of course, that we will not be opening the lab until after lunch," Professor Calvin said. All the geeks groaned. "Due to an unfortunate chemical leak—er, mishap—in the basement."

"Bummer," said Miranda with a grin.

Lizzie helped herself to another muffin. Today was starting off a lot better than yesterday. And, hey, maybe she'd get to spend some quality time with Devon!

Less than an hour later, Lizzie was looking around at her Cabin Silver Nitrate scavenger team.

Great, Lizzie thought. A whole morning with Kate and Claire. And Sunny, of course, our clueless leader. At the moment, the counselor was busy trying to help a hungry slug onto a maple leaf.

At least, Miranda was there. And Gordo, who had volunteered to join them since Cabin Potassium Chloride had a larger head count. He was carrying his briefcase by a strap over his shoulder.

Judy and Trudy, the two science nerds, were part of the Silver Nitrate team, too.

"Okay, let's get this over with," Miranda said.

Lizzie sighed and began to read off the list they'd been given. "A pinecone, a nonpoisonous mushroom, a fern leaf." She paused. "A piece of birch bark from the ground, not the tree—"

Kate rolled her eyes in disgust. "This is so dumb," she said. "We had to find the same stupid stuff in kindergarten."

"A chip of mica, a rock with quartz in it, a slug . . ." Lizzie went on.

Claire bent down and swooped Sunny's hungry slug off its maple leaf. "Check one off," she snapped coolly. Then she tossed the slimy creature at Trudy, who popped it into a jar on her belt.

Kate shuddered. "Claire, how could you touch that gross, slimy thing?"

Claire shrugged. "Anything to speed up this dorky exercise."

Lizzie couldn't help being disappointed that she wasn't in Devon's group. And she couldn't keep an eye on Tudgeman, either. But at least Gordo's formula was safe.

Every once in a while they ran into other groups. Professor Calvin was leading Matt's cabin. Devon was with Potassium Chloride, of course. Once or twice, when the she-geeks were arguing over various plant species, Lizzie borrowed Judy's binoculars so she could catch a glimpse of Devon through the trees.

"Hey, here's something interesting!" Sunny called. She hauled up a shiny-looking plant with three leaves.

"Don't touch that!" Gordo warned. Sunny was already brushing her hair off her forehead, still holding the plant. Gordo winced. "It's poison ivy!"

Sunny's eyes widened. "Ohhhh. Not good," she said, scratching her face. "Well, that's what I get for specializing in the heavens—a dis from the jealous earth! I'm actually starting to itch already. You kids wait right here, okay? I'm going to see if I can borrow a first-aid kit from Devon's group. Don't move from this spot."

"This is boring," Kate said after Sunny had been gone for a total of two minutes. "Let's keep walking."

"We can't," Lizzie said. "Sunny wants us to stay here."

Suddenly, there was a loud whirring sound from the trees behind them.

Everyone froze.

"What's that?" Claire whispered.

"Maybe it's the ghost of the creepy caretaker," Miranda said.

"You're not serious!" cried Lizzie. "It's bad enough Matt believed that story."

"Chill, Lizzie," said Miranda. "I was just kidding. Sort of . . ."

The sound grew louder and louder.

"Definitely something mechanical," Gordo said, frowning. He held his briefcase tighter.

"Like what?" asked Claire. Even Ms. Cool Slug Wrangler was beginning to look nervous.

"Like a *chain saw* or something?" Kate said.

Everyone exchanged glances. This time no one, not even Miranda, looked amused.

"Run!" cried Kate.

Team Silver Nitrate immediately raced away from the whirring sound. As they ran deeper into the woods, Lizzie and Kate both ran smack into something large and solid. It was dangling from a rope hung over a tree branch.

"Ow," Lizzie said, rubbing her head.

"Ohmigosh!" Kate shrieked. "It's a body!"

"What?" Lizzie said in alarm.

"No joke," Kate said, her voice rising.

Lizzie took another look as the others came up. "It's not a body," she said slowly. "It's a scarecrow. And it's wearing a Camp Bunsen Burner T-shirt."

Kate threw up her hands. "Well, no surprise there," she said. "This whole place is a horror show." She looked around nervously. "Is that chain-saw thing *gone*?"

"Sounds like it's headed toward the lake," Miranda said. "I think."

Lizzie took another step toward the scarecrow. There was a note pinned to its T-shirt.

"'Don't go near the lake,'" Gordo read over her shoulder. "Once again, a classic camp horror flick. Obviously, some kind of a joke."

"Not so fast, Gor-dork," Kate said. "Read the small print."

Lizzie tried to block Gordo's view, but it was too late. The tiny letters below the warning read: THAT MEANS YOU, GORDO!

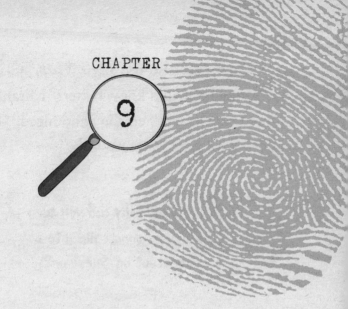

9

"ME?!" Gordo cried. "Why can't *I* go near the lake?" He clutched his briefcase and gazed around the woods.

The scarecrow in the Camp Bunsen Burner T-shirt stared down at him, looking evil.

"It's okay, Gordo," Lizzie said, leading him away from the tree. "Like you said, it's just a joke."

Lizzie wanted to investigate and get a better look at the handwriting on the threatening note. But helping her friend was more important right now.

"Whoa, this is so-o-o *Blair Witch*," Claire said.

"And who would know better?" Miranda murmured to Lizzie. Then she announced, "Let's get out of here. This is Creep City."

Mom? Dad? Why did you turn your only *good* child into a contestant on *Survivor*?!

Kate looked around. "Okay, which way do we go?" she said. "These stupid trees all look the same."

"We should wait for Sunny," Judy said.

Kate looked at her as if she was the slug in Trudy's belt jar. "Sunny is not coming back."

True, Lizzie thought. Maybe that poison-ivy deal was just a trick. Sunny ran ahead and put the scarecrow here to freak us all out.

None of the other suspects had been around. Or had they? Lizzie sighed. It was impossible to keep an eye on Tudgeman and Professor Calvin in the woods. Even with binoculars.

"I think we're south of camp. So we should travel north. You can tell which way is north by the moss—it grows on the north side of the tree," Trudy said shyly.

"Great," Kate said. "Which direction is the camp?"

Trudy looked around. "Lack of data prevents me from answering that question."

Kate threw up her hands in disgust. "Well, I'm walking this way," she said.

Lizzie fumbled in her knapsack. "Wait a sec," she said. She pulled out a pocket-sized copy of *The Non-Hiker's Guide to the Universe.* "Maybe this will help."

"Whoa, McGuire," Claire said. "You really are a geek."

Thanks again, Mom, Lizzie thought. She skimmed the book. "Okay, what time is it? We can use the height of the sun to find north."

Gordo checked his watch. "It's noon," he said. "So that won't work. The sun is in the middle of the sky."

"I hate this place," Miranda said. "Let's start walking. Somewhere. Anywhere."

"Okay," Lizzie said. She pointed back at the scarecrow. "Let's go back and retrace our steps. That should be easy."

Half an hour later, the Silver Nitrate scavenger team was still totally lost. "Sorry, guys," Lizzie said, sighing. "All these paths with the weird vines over them look the same."

Everyone looked too exhausted, sweaty, and dirty to care. Except Kate. "You're a loser, McGuire. *This* way." She raced off through the trees. Claire followed her.

Lizzie looked around at the rest of the team. "Guess we might as well go the same direction as Kate," she said. "We all should at least try to stay together."

Gordo adjusted his briefcase. By now, he was

really getting sick of lugging it around. "Let's boogie," he said, and they started walking.

But Kate had rushed so far ahead, Lizzie couldn't see her. After a while Lizzie stopped. "Do you hear that?" she asked. "I think it's water."

"The lake," Miranda said. "Someone's splashing around."

Gordo frowned. "I don't think the lake is a good idea," he said, remembering that personalized little warning to stay *away* from the lake. "Let's get out of here."

"But the lake is the way we can find our way out of this maze," Lizzie told him. "Once we get to it, we can follow the edge of it back to the cabins."

Just then, there was a scream. It was Claire. "Help!" Claire cried. "Kate's drowning!"

Gordo bolted to help, and Lizzie and the others followed, rushing toward the sound of Claire's voice. Sure enough, Kate was splashing around in the lake, next to an overturned canoe. Claire was trying to hold on to the canoe and pull Kate onto it. There was a second, empty canoe floating beside them.

"Whoa," Miranda said. "Maybe there really *is* something to that caretaker's ghost story!"

Just as Gordo was about to jump in, something jettisoned Kate out of the water and onto the canoe next to Claire. Another head appeared above the water, gasping for breath.

It was Devon!

He swam over and helped Kate and Claire back into the canoe. Kate seemed fine now. She just looked mad.

"What were you doing, holding me underwater?" she said to Devon. "I was perfectly okay until *you* showed up."

Kate's *yelling* at Devon? i knew the Evil Queen couldn't keep her witch warts masked for long. But this must be some kind of record. *Whoo-hoo!* He's all *mine!*

Devon calmly got into the other canoe and started paddling toward shore. "There are some pretty gnarly weeds in this lake," Lizzie heard him say to Kate over his shoulder. "Your legs must have gotten stuck."

He pulled the canoe back on shore, where most of his team was waiting. Lizzie noticed that "Doctor" Tudgeman and his "loyal assistant" Ethan weren't there. "You girls shouldn't have taken the canoe out alone," Devon said.

Claire dragged herself out of the water. "We were just trying to have some fun." She shaded her eyes and looked back at the boys' sports camp across the lake. "So close . . . and yet so far."

"Well, we would have been fine if you hadn't come out and capsized us in the first place," Kate told Devon. She was dripping wet—and still hopping mad.

Just then, Professor Calvin burst through the woods with Matt and Malina's group. He was carrying his chimp, Alonzo—and Sunny was trailing behind them, looking confused.

"The junior campers have won the Camp Bunsen Burner Scientific Scavenger Hunt!" the professor announced. "And it's time to celebrate with a victory lunch!"

"Uh-oh," said Gordo.

"What?" asked Lizzie. Her best friend had gone pale.

"My briefcase," said Gordo. "The strap must have broken while I was running to help Kate."

Just then, Professor Calvin came up to Lizzie, Miranda, and Gordo. He smiled and handed Gordo his briefcase. "Found this in the woods, young man," he said. "I believe it's yours."

Gordo looked stunned. "Um, thanks," he said.

Just as Gordo had guessed, the metal loop holding the leather strap to the briefcase part had broken. The thing had probably been super-stressed from Gordo's lugging it everywhere 24/7, Lizzie told herself.

As soon as the professor walked away, Gordo

looked inside the briefcase. With a sigh of relief he told Lizzie and Miranda, "Everything's cool. My notes are still here."

"Great," Lizzie said. She tried not to let Gordo see how worried she was. Professor Calvin could have looked at the notes.

As for her other suspects, Tudgeman and Ethan were AWOL. And who knew where Sunny had been? Her brush with the poison ivy could have been a setup—an excuse to get away from the group and set some booby traps.

Just then, Lizzie spotted Tudgeman and Ethan lugging the heavy duffel along the lake. *Aha!* Had they been in the woods the whole time? And what had been making that crazy whirring sound?

This case was getting stranger by the minute.

CHAPTER

10

"So, girls!" Professor Calvin said cheerfully to Lizzie and Miranda later that afternoon. The two of them were sitting on stools in the science lab, feeling totally miserable. "I understand you don't have a project idea for the big Expo."

"Um, not yet, Professor Calvin," Lizzie said. She smiled weakly.

"Excellent!" the professor said. "Do I have the perfect project for you."

He brought his hand out from behind his

back and held out something large and hairy—
with teeth and claws and a long tail.

"Aaaahhh!" Miranda cried, jumping off her
stool. "What is that . . . thing?"

Lizzie drew back as Professor Calvin brought
the squirming creature closer. "It's a Mongolian
gerbil," he said. "We raise them right here at
Camp Bunsen Burner. And you girls can have
the golden opportunity of teaching them to run
a simple maze."

How about something a little
more appealing? Like, say,
collecting mold from the dining
hall and watching it grow?

Professor Calvin led the girls to a small room
down the hall. All four walls were lined with
plastic cages filled with gerbils.

Lizzie shut her eyes as the professor explained

how to run the little animals through the maze.

"Observe each movement they make and write it down on your clipboard," he said. "You'll also need a stopwatch, of course, to measure their progress."

Professor Calvin went on and on with his instructions. Lizzie hoped Miranda was listening. At the moment, her best friend's eyes looked sort of glazed.

Lizzie's own thoughts turned to Gordo, who was working in a private lab down the hall. Was someone still after his formula? Or *him*?

"So, I'll leave you scientists alone now to begin your study," Professor Calvin finally finished. Lizzie was jolted back to the horrifying reality of the gerbil room. "Good luck, girls!" he called on his way out the door.

Miranda sighed. "Might as well get this over with," she said.

She closed her eyes, reached into one of the plastic cages and pulled out a little squirmy gerbil. With a shudder, she placed it in the wooden maze set up on the floor. "Run, rat, run!" she said in a high, squeaky voice.

"Um, Miranda, I hate to ask you this," Lizzie said. "But do you mind if I do a little investigating here in the lab?"

Miranda leaned closer to the maze. The gerbil was standing on its hind legs, sniffing the air. "You know, he's actually kind of cute," she said. Then she made some kissy sounds. "How about I name you Brad?"

"Brad?" said Lizzie.

"As in Brad Pitt," said Miranda. "He's sort of got Brad's eyes, don't you think?"

Lizzie just stared at her friend.

Is it me? Or is this place sending Miranda over the edge?

"Go ahead, Lizzie," said Miranda. "Brad and I will be just fine here."

"Thanks," Lizzie said. "Um . . . I'll be *right* back. I'm just going to check on Gordo for one sec."

Miranda pulled a lettuce leaf off a dish next to the plastic cages. She tore off a piece and held it up for Brad. "No problem. Take your time. Here, little Brad, here you go . . ."

As Miranda made more kissy noises, Lizzie hurried down the hall toward Gordo's lab. She really wanted to make this a quick trip—she was beginning to worry about Miranda!

The hallway was empty as she walked swiftly along. Framed pictures of scientists and various inventors lined the walls: Albert Einstein, Thomas Edison, Marie Curie, the Wright Brothers, then a whole lotta people she didn't recognize . . . Lizzie moved faster, hoping she wasn't going to encounter Dr. Frankenstein holding up a corpse with bolts in its neck.

Then she passed Professor Calvin's office—

and stopped. The door was open, and she could hear the professor's raised voice.

"Please reconsider, Mr. Gecko. Alonzo is making great strides. We just need more time. . . ."

Lizzie flattened herself against the wall to listen. Then she peered around the door. Professor Calvin was on the phone. He looked upset.

"But, Mr. Gecko, the loss of your generous funding will be a disaster. And I own Camp Bunsen Burner, as you know. Without more money for research . . ."

Hmmmm, Lizzie thought. Why would Professor Calvin wreck his own camp's reputation if he needs money? He wouldn't want to scare kids away and risk parents' demanding their money back. And he sure wouldn't want to keep Gordo from presenting his big project at the Science Expo. It was great publicity.

"Yes, Mr. Gecko," Professor Calvin said. "Just a little more time. I'll deliver the research as soon as the campers are gone."

Whoa! Lizzie realized. Professor Calvin basically just said he wants us all out of the way.

Suddenly, a familiar whirring noise came from somewhere down the hall.

I *have* to find out what that thing is, Lizzie told herself. I'll check on Professor Calvin later.

The whirring noise grew louder as Lizzie tore down the hall. She stopped at the third door on the right and threw it open.

There was nothing there. But the whirring was getting even louder now.

Suddenly, Lizzie was pushed forward—and the door slammed behind her.

"Hey!" she cried. "Who did that? Let me out! Right *now*!"

As she struggled with the doorknob, she hit a switch on the wall. A faint light came from a red lightbulb. Lizzie realized she was in a storage closet. Shelves were packed with boxes, tubes, beakers—

And a grinning skeleton!

11

"Okay, don't panic," Lizzie told herself. She backed away from the skeleton and started pounding frantically on the storage closet door again.

"Help!" she screamed. "Get me *out* of here!"

Suddenly, the door flew open. Lizzie stumbled out of the closet and fell onto the floor. The skeleton crashed down on top of her.

"EEEEK!" Lizzie cried as the skeleton's bony hand brushed her face.

"Relax, Lizzie," a voice said. "It's just one of those learn-anatomy dummies."

Lizzie stared up at—Larry Tudgeman?

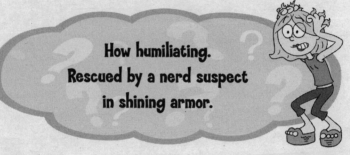

How humiliating. Rescued by a nerd suspect in shining armor.

Tudgeman helped Lizzie up. "Are you okay?" he asked.

"I guess so," Lizzie said, brushing herself off. She was covered in cobwebs and dust.

"What were you doing, anyway?" Tudgeman said. "Sneaking around?" His eyes narrowed. "Spying on me, perhaps? Trying to find out about my top-secret project?"

Lizzie glared at him. "You know, Larry, I don't have time for this. What do you know about that weird, whirring machine-thing?"

Tudgeman looked nervously down the hall. "I

have no idea what you're talking about," he said. Lizzie noticed beads of sweat forming on his upper lip. "You know, what, Lizzie? Sometimes you're a little too nosy for your own good."

First, I'm too perky; now, I'm too nosy, Lizzie thought. Sounds like the Tudge has something to hide.

Tudgeman suddenly leaned in close to Lizzie. "Mind your own beeswax, okay?" he said. Then he took off down the hall.

Go ahead and run. But you're still at the top of my suspect list! . . . You and three other people.

Just then, a door flew open at the end of the hall. Gordo ran toward Lizzie. "It's gone!" he shouted. "I'm ruined!"

"What's gone?" Lizzie asked in alarm. "Your briefcase?"

Gordo grabbed both sides of his head in panic. "My briefcase is still on the counter where I left it. But someone took all my notes—and a test tube of my latest batch of Skeeter-Killer Glow Gel!"

"Okay, Gordo, chill," Lizzie said. "We'll find it. And we'll find the culprit, too. You stay here. I'll get Miranda to help us."

She rushed back to the gerbil room. Miranda was curled up on the floor next to the maze, fast asleep. Brad was nibbling on her pom-pom hair band. Two other critters were running crazily through the maze, bumping into the walls and each other.

"Miranda, wake up!" Lizzie said, shaking her friend. "It's a Gordo 9-1-1!"

Lizzie, Miranda, and Gordo put the gerbils back into their cages. Then they raced to the room where Gordo had been working and searched every inch of it.

"*Nada*," Lizzie said with a sigh. "Nothing. Not

a single clue. Gordo, are you sure no one came in here? What about Tudgeman?"

Gordo shook his head. "I don't think so. Devon stopped in for a second, but he's checking in on all of us. I might have heard that whirring thing out in the hall once or twice. I guess I was really concentrating on refining the combination of elements in my formula."

Suddenly, the whole room seemed to shake, as a series of loud explosions sounded from across the hall.

Lizzie, Miranda, and Gordo ducked and covered their heads, waiting for the worst.

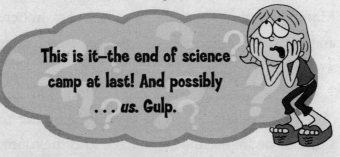

This is it—the end of science camp at last! And possibly . . . *us.* Gulp.

Finally, the explosions stopped. The door across the hall opened, and Matt McGuire walked out, dazed. He was covered from spiky head to sneakers in debris.

"Matt!" Lizzie cried in alarm, rushing toward her little brother.

"Don't worry," Matt said. "I'm fine." He sighed heavily. "But I fear I have failed."

"What happened?" Lizzie asked.

"A little testing of the ol' Five-Step Scientific Method," Matt told her. "Let's just say . . . my hypothesis did not match my conclusion."

Malina emerged from the junior chem lab, removing her goggles. Not a single blond hair on her head was out of place. "You really blew it, Matt McGuire," she said. "Now, get back in here and get this whole mess cleaned up. Right now, so we can try again as soon as possible."

"Yes, my little Marie Curie," Matt told her. "Isn't she brilliant?" he said over his shoulder to Lizzie as he followed Malina back into the room.

"Sorry, Gordo, I'll be right back," Lizzie said. "I have to see what's going on in there."

"We'll come with you," Miranda said.

To Lizzie's surprise, Sunny was standing in the middle of the room, frowning. "I can't believe it turned out like this," she said. "Don't worry, Lizzie, the kids are okay. I've been watching them every second."

Huh, Lizzie thought. Looks like Sunny might be off the suspect hook. For now, anyway. She looked around. "What were you guys *doing*?"

"Oh, rigging one of those stupid erupting volcano deals," Malina said. She smiled. "With a few extra bangs."

"We must have mixed something wrong," Sunny said. "Sorry."

Hmm, Lizzie thought. Was this all a distraction devised by Ms. Star Power? Could she have ducked out to steal Gordo's formula?

Negative, Lizzie reminded herself. The formula was stolen *before* the explosions.

Gordo stepped forward. "I'll help you guys out," he said. "I'm a pro at exploding volcanoes.

I made a working model of Mount Vesuvius in kindergarten."

When the volcano experiment seemed safely under control, Lizzie, Gordo, and Miranda went back to Gordo's lab.

"Let's take one more look," Lizzie said. "We must have missed something." She stopped at the door. "Wait a second. Who turned off the lights?"

"I did," Gordo said. "I hit the switch when the explosions went off." He shrugged. "Standard chemical emergency evacuation procedure. Safety first."

"There's something gooey on the floor," Lizzie said. "And . . . *glowing*."

"That's my formula," Gordo said. "It only shows up in the dark. Looks like there's a whole *trail* of it."

"Okay," Lizzie said. "Follow that formula!"

"We'll have to turn the lights out in the hall," Lizzie said. "Or we won't be able to see the formula trail glow."

"I think there's a light switch near Professor Calvin's office," Gordo said. He jogged down the hall.

Devon stepped out of a lab room in front of Lizzie and Miranda. "Hey, what are you two doing? Aren't you supposed to be in the gerbil room?"

"We're looking for—" Miranda began.

Lizzie nudged her friend and frowned.

No matter how cute the guy is, this investigation is top secret! Like Gordo's formula *used* to be. Sigh.

"We're just testing out the Five-Step Scientific Method," Lizzie told Devon.

"Great," Devon said. "Always a favorite of mine. Use it all the time."

Miranda threw up her hands. "Okay, shoot me. What *is* the stupid Five-Step Scientific Method?"

Devon grinned. "Hey, come on. You know it."

Miranda thought for a second. "Nope. Doesn't ring a bell."

"I know," Lizzie said eagerly. Here was her chance to impress Devon. "Hypothesis, Observation, Experimentation, and Conclusion. No, wait. Experimentation comes before Observation. I think."

"That's only four," Miranda said.

Thanks so much for pointing that out, Lizzie told her friend silently. She turned to Devon. "Oops," she said. "I give up. What is the fifth one again?"

Devon raised his eyebrows. "Well, it's, uh . . . *hmm*, hold on a sec." He hit the side of his head jokingly. "Guess I can't remember, either. You should look that up." He smiled and headed down the hall. "I've got to get back to work. And you two should get back to those gerbils."

"Come on, you guys," Gordo called impatiently. "Let's go!" He switched off the hall light.

Lizzie and Miranda made their way back toward Gordo. Luckily, there were drops of green Skeeter-Killer Glow Gel to guide them down the dark hallway.

Lizzie glanced inside Professor Calvin's office as they passed. He didn't seem to notice that the lights were out in the hall. His face was buried in his hands. Alonzo sat on the desk beside him, patting the professor on the shoulder.

Lizzie paused. Professor Calvin seemed really, really upset. Was he actually . . . *crying*?

"Um, Professor?" Lizzie asked gently. "Is everything okay?"

Professor Calvin looked up. "No, my dear," he said sadly. "Everything is *not* okay. Alonzo and I have lost our funding. My scientific career has gone down the drain. And I'm going to have to close my beloved Camp Bunsen Burner!"

"No great loss," Miranda whispered behind Lizzie.

But Lizzie felt really sorry for the professor. He seemed genuinely brokenhearted. She glanced back at the hallway.

The glowing footsteps led straight past Professor Calvin's door.

Looks like another suspect off the hook, Lizzie thought. "I'm sure everything will be all right.

Just don't give up," she told the professor. "Gotta get back to work on the case. I mean, the gerbils."

As she stepped back into the hall, Lizzie heard something familiar ahead of her. That crazy whirring sound.

"Stay on the glow trail. We can't lose it!" Lizzie told Miranda and Gordo.

"Righto, detective," Miranda said, giving Lizzie a salute.

Lizzie, Gordo, and Miranda quickly followed the glowing footsteps the rest of the way down the long, dark hall. They led around the corner and—straight into Tudgeman and Ethan.

"**O**kay, guys," Lizzie said to Tudgeman and his partner in crime. "It's time to come clean."

"*Huh?*" Tudgeman said, blinking in the shadows.

Ethan shook his head. "Lizzie, Lizzie, Lizzie. What do you mean?" He looked pleased. "Hey, that rhymes. You know, with clean. Cool."

"Impressive," Gordo said with a raised eyebrow.

"So what are you two up to?" Lizzie asked. She looked down at the bulky duffel that Tudgeman and Ethan had been trying to lug out of the lab building. "Going somewhere in a hurry?"

"Gee, there must be some important stuff in there," Miranda said. "Like, say, a top secret project for the Science Expo. Or maybe even . . . *two* projects."

Lizzie saw Tudgeman begin to twitch again. Then he made a sudden move for the duffel and tried to make a break for the door. Gordo immediately grabbed him.

"Dude, what's the deal?" Ethan said. Lizzie wasn't sure whether he was talking to Tudgeman or Gordo. He just seemed . . . confused.

Unfortunately, "confused" is sort of Ethan's biologically natural state. It's hard to think of him as suspicious.

Lizzie reached to unzip the bag.

"Get away from there!" Tudgeman yelled.

"Zip it, Tudgeman," said Gordo, holding him back.

"Hear that?" Lizzie announced as she opened the bag. The whirring was getting louder the more she unzipped. "It's that weird machine thing."

She peered into the duffel, then jumped back.

"AAAAAHHHH!" Lizzie screamed. A hideous, scary-looking robot face stared back at her.

Now, there's a mechanical creature even George Lucas couldn't love!

"I don't know what this robot thing is," she told Tudgeman. "But where's Gordo's formula? It's leaking out of your bag, you know."

"Formula? Leaking?" Tudgeman knelt down beside the duffel and pulled it completely out. "Is my robot being corroded?"

"We'll tell you if you tell us," Lizzie said as Larry anxiously circled his mechanical creation, examining every inch of it.

"It *looks* okay," mumbled Tudgeman.

"What's the story, Tudgeman?" said Lizzie. "Spill it."

The Tudge's shoulders slumped. He looked totally defeated.

"You're looking at a reconnaissance robot," he told them.

"Ex-squeeze me?" said Lizzie.

"It's a droid that retrieves data from a remote position and returns it to the operator," Gordo told her. "Recon robots are what scientists use to go places people can't. Like it can go inside the crater of a volcano that's about to erupt and measure seismic activity—"

Tudgeman interrupted Gordo. "*My* version is intended for *commercial* use," he explained. "For regular people."

"What are we supposed to use it for?" asked

Gordo skeptically. "Spying on our families?"

"I was thinking more of a golfer who might want to improve his swing. Take this little baby along and you've got a recording of your entire game. Or, say, for a wedding or family reunion— my reconnaissance robot could drift around the room recording different aspects of the event."

"I see." Gordo nodded, impressed. "Not bad, Tudgeman."

"Except I didn't want it to be revealed before the Science Expo," said the Tudge with a sigh. "It still has a few . . . bugs."

"Bugs?" Miranda said. She stepped back nervously.

"It escapes a lot," Tudgeman said. "It seems intent on completing its own self-guided missions. I've had my hands full trying to keep up with it."

Lizzie frowned. "Wait a minute. You mean—?"

Tudgeman nodded sadly. "I've been chasing my own science project all over camp."

"So that's what those whirring sounds were," Lizzie said slowly. "Outside my cabin and in the woods and the lab and—"

"Yes," Tudgeman said. "I'm afraid so."

His story does sound pretty believable, Lizzie thought. But still . . . "Guys, lift up your feet," she said.

Tudgeman and Ethan exchanged puzzled glances. But Tudgeman raised one sneaker and then the other. Ethan did the same with his flip-flops.

Okay, no glowing goo, Lizzie told herself. But when she checked the robot, she found traces of Skeeter-Killer Glow Gel on its wheels.

She turned toward Gordo. But he was already in deep discussion with Tudgeman about the robot.

"Are you using a digital camera?" asked Gordo.

Tudgeman shook his head. "No. My next upgrade will have a DVD burner. This is just the first prototype. It uses videotape."

"The DVD burner would be sweet," said Gordo.

"Yeah," he said, "and the design needs some tweaking, too. My ultimate plan is to model it on the greatest robot of all time, R2-D2."

Miranda rolled her eyes. "Great," she said under her breath. "Looks like Obi-Wan Kenobi is our only hope."

"Hey, wait a minute," Lizzie said. "Maybe Tudgeman's invention *can* help us find the formula thief!"

"Huh?" Miranda said.

Lizzie turned to Tudgeman. "You said your robot's function is to take pictures, right?"

"Right," he said.

Lizzie knelt down, Princess Leia style, and examined the belly of the robot. She peered into the camera's eye. "Can it play back what it records?" she asked.

"No," said Larry. "But you can play the tape in any standard video unit."

Lizzie pressed a small red EJECT button and the panel opened to reveal the videotape.

Move over, Tudgeman! i am now officially a technological genius.

"C'mon," said Lizzie. "Follow me."

Lizzie led everyone to the front of an empty lecture room. She popped the tape into the video machine there and rewound it a little. Then she played the tape and, sure enough, the TV screen showed someone looking both ways as they stepped out a door. The person was carrying a folder stuffed with notepads and index cards—and a beaker full of steaming liquid.

There was no doubt about it. The spy robot had caught the Skeeter-Killer Glow Gel formula thief *green*-handed!

"I can't believe it!" Lizzie said. She played the robot's tape again. This time she put it on pause. "It's Devon."

"I can't believe my eyes," Miranda said. "He's too nice . . . and too *cute.*"

Lizzie pointed to the tape and shrugged. "There's the evidence. It's him, all right. Take another look, everyone."

The others leaned in as Lizzie played the tape one more time.

"*Whoa,*" said Gordo.

"Inconceivable," said Tudgeman.

"Bogus," said Ethan.

Lizzie sighed.

it's not true what they say that cameras never lie. *Lie, lie, lie,* you miserable waste of metal! Um, *please?*

"I guess a lot of clues pointed to Devon all along," Lizzie said. "I just didn't realize it until a few minutes ago."

She started to count on her fingers. "*One,* Devon was on the bus for the smoke bomb, so he could have set it off. And he was the last one *off* the bus, too. He was probably trying to steal Gordo's formula right from the start."

"But he didn't even know what my project was," Gordo said. "No one did."

Miranda shook her head. "You did stand up

and announce to the whole bus that you had the greatest discovery of all time in that briefcase."

"*Two*, Devon was Gordo's counselor," Lizzie went on. "He could have stolen one of Sunny's star charts on the bus and marked it with that threatening message, which would also frame Sunny at the same time. And he could have put the jar on one of the beds in Cabin Silver Nitrate, which was right next door."

"True," Miranda said, nodding. "But what was the reason for the pickled frog incident?"

"Just another way to freak out Gordo," said Lizzie. "Obviously, Devon put Gordo's name on the frog jar and then scared Kate with it to try getting Gordo into trouble. Devon was probably trying to intimidate him into leaving camp before he could present his formula to the world at the Science Expo. Which brings me to *three*: he obviously followed Gordo one night to my cabin, then hid in the dark, listening to Gordo tell me about his formula. He only turned on his flashlight and told us he was on night duty *after* Gordo started coming toward him with my lantern."

"*Four*, Devon was always asking Gordo and Larry about their projects. And *five*, Devon could have rigged the scarecrow in the woods ahead of time," Lizzie finshed.

"Um, you're wrong there," said Tudgeman.

"Why?" asked Lizzie. But she immediately guessed the answer the second she saw Tudgeman redden with embarrassment.

"*You* put the scarecrow up, didn't you, Tudgeman?" said Lizzie. "To keep Gordo and everyone else away from the lake."

Tudgeman shrugged. "I was still testing my robot, and I wanted to do it in privacy."

"So that whole thing with Kate at the lake wasn't a setup?" asked Gordo.

"No," Tudgeman said, "just a coincidence."

"More like a dumb cheer-queen," Lizzie pointed out.

"Well, I guess that makes sense," said Gordo.

"No one could have known for sure that my briefcase would break."

"Okay, fine," said Lizzie, "so that incident was a red herring."

Miranda frowned. "Red herring? What does smoked fish have to do with your suspect?"

"Detective-speak," Lizzie explained. "A red herring is a false clue."

"Ahh," said Miranda. "Well, it still sounds weird."

Lizzie paused for breath. "Okay, where was I?"

"Number five," said Gordo.

"Right. Well . . ." Lizzie looked at her hand. "I'm running out of fingers," she said with a shrug. "But I'm betting Devon's the thief."

"I guess the fingers do point to him," Gordo said. "But here's the million-dollar jackpot question: *Why* would Devon want my formula? He can't enter the Camp Bunsen Burner Science Expo. He's a counselor."

"And he's *already* been published in *American*

Scientific Journal," Tudgeman added. "He must be some kind of prodigy."

"Well, there was one other very important clue," Lizzie said slowly. "Devon didn't know the Five-Step Scientific Method. He was totally stumped when I asked him about the fifth step. Even my stupid little brother knows that."

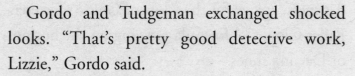

Ladies and gentlemen of the jury, I rest my case!

Gordo and Tudgeman exchanged shocked looks. "That's pretty good detective work, Lizzie," Gordo said.

"Stellar," Tudgeman agreed.

"Wait. Then are you saying Devon is some kind of a . . . scientific fraud?" Miranda asked.

"Well, I don't know for sure," Lizzie said. "But we're about to find out."

* * *

Lizzie and the others confronted Devon in the counselors' lounge. He sat on the couch with his feet propped up on the coffee table, studying a textbook.

"Business Deals 101?" Miranda whispered, reading the title. "Isn't he supposed to be a *science* major?"

"Hi, Devon," Lizzie said. "It's kind of bright in here. Mind if we turn off the lights?"

Devon looked up in surprise. Before he could answer, Lizzie flipped the switch.

The counselors' lounge was plunged into darkness. *Except* for the spots of Gordo's Skeeter-Killer Glow Gel formula glowing on the bottom of Devon's shoes.

Lizzie sighed. "This may hurt me as much as it hurts you, Devon," she said. "But you are totally busted."

"I *had* to do it," said Devon. "I was desperate!"

After half an hour of tough interrogation—and a quick rescreening of the robot's video-tape—the Skeeter-Killer Glow Gel thief had finally broken down. Now the hottie counselor tried to give Lizzie and her friends his trademark megawatt smile.

"Sorry," Lizzie told him. "Charm won't work this time." She crossed her arms. "There's one thing I can't figure out. *Why* did you do it, Devon?"

Devon tried to peel the sticky formula off the bottom of his shoes. "Well, my science grades were a bit on the low side last semester. I lost my scholarship."

"But what about that brilliant paper you wrote for *American Scientific Journal*?" Gordo said.

Devon shrugged. "Bought it off the Internet."

"Pathetic," Tudgeman said.

"I wanted to switch to a business major, but then I'd have to pay the tuition myself." Devon smiled charmingly. "I figured if I could patent some really amazing invention, the bucks would just roll in. And that's the key to business, right?"

"I don't think that's exactly how it works," Lizzie said.

Devon turned to Gordo. "So you have the brains, and I have the marketing skills," he said. "What do you say we make a deal?"

"Tell me you're kidding," Gordo said.

"Hey," Devon said as Lizzie and her friends escorted him from the counselors' lounge. "I'm not a bad person. Honest."

"Tell that to the professor," Lizzie said.

The Camp Bunsen Burner Science Expo was a big success. All the parents were there, along with the reporter from *Future Scientists of America* magazine. The campers got to show off their projects, and Alonzo was a big hit with the crowd. Professor Calvin looked very happy.

"Too bad about your formula, Gordo," Lizzie said.

Gordo shook his head and said, "Who could have known?"

While Gordo's Skeeter-Killer Glow Gel did *repel* mosquitoes, it unfortunately also *attracted* bees. Swarms of them came at him from Judy and Trudy's "Secrets from the Honeycomb" exhibit. Lucky for Gordo, the girls were expert bee handlers—so his stings were minor.

Tudgeman and Ethan didn't fare any better than Gordo. Their robot kept crashing into the tables, knocking campers' projects to the floor.

"Looks like they programmed that thing to destroy," Miranda noted.

Lizzie glanced down at the floor. "Well, I don't think our project is too a-*maze*-ing, either," she said. "Those gerbils are trying to escape again. Even little Brad."

Mrs. McGuire patted Lizzie's shoulder and said, "Don't worry, honey. You did your best. That's what's important. And you had fun, too."

Lizzie and Miranda exchanged glances. "Um, right, Mom," Lizzie said.

When the Camp Bunsen Burner Science Expo grand prize was announced, Matt and Malina were the surprise winners. With a little help from Professor Calvin, they'd turned their erupting volcano into a supersonic wave pool model.

"Perfect for surfing," Lizzie overheard Matt telling the *Future Scientists of America* reporter.

Matt leaned closer. "Confidentially, Professor Calvin already has offers from investors to turn this place into a water park for next summer. *Very* lucrative possibilities."

Mrs. McGuire turned to Lizzie. "Honey, is that really true?" she whispered.

Lizzie shrugged. With her little brother's history of exaggeration—like telling Lizzie's entire class how he'd made a film with Steven Spielberg and taught Britney Spears to dance—Lizzie could never be sure *anything* Matt said was true. On the other hand, Professor Calvin had never looked happier.

"I don't know, Mom," said Lizzie. "I just don't know."

"Well, your brother *is* full of surprises," said Mrs. McGuire. "Either way, maybe next year you and your friends can come back and—"

Lizzie looked at Miranda and Gordo. "Sorry, Mom," she said, "but no thanks. Count us *outie!*"

Lizzie McGuire MYSTERIES

Want to have a way cool time? Here's a clue. . . . Read the next Lizzie McGuire Mystery!

Case of THE MISSING SHE-GEEK

In a (failed) effort to be cool in school, Lizzie hurts the feelings of major she-geek Audrey Albright. It's a total mistake and Lizzie wants to apologize—but Audrey's disappeared. She was last seen crying in the girls' room. And Lizzie can't find her anywhere! So who's got the 4-1-1 on the missing Audrey? With Gordo and Miranda in tow, Lizzie follows a trail of clues to a science-fiction convention, where Larry Tudgeman may be her only guide through the underworld of geekdom. But is Lizzie really ready to go where no cool kid (like, ever!) has gone before?

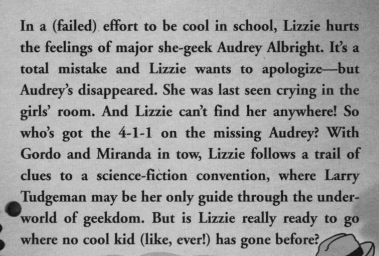

"Missing person? i'm all over it!"